MAXX TRAX II

MONSTER TRUCK ADVENTURE

by James Preller

Illustrated by Don Bolognese

SCHOLASTIC INC.

New York   Toronto   London   Auckland   Sydney

For Evan and Timmy,
who would probably be Monster Trucks,
if they weren't already boys.
—J. P.

To my '72 Land Rover
—D. B.

ISBN 0-590-41156-X

Text copyright © 1988 by James Preller.
Illustrations copyright © 1988 by Don Bolognese.
All rights reserved. Published by Scholastic Inc.
Art direction by Diana Hrisinko.

12 11 10 9 8 7 6 5 4 3 2 1   8 9/8 0 1 2 3/9

Printed in the U.S.A.   23
First Scholastic printing, February 1988

DEEP IN A remote mountain range,
far from man and lost in time,
a secret research group developed
a special breed of superpowered trucks.
Bigger, stronger, and more advanced than
any vehicles the world has ever seen,
these mighty trucks are known as
MAXX TRAX.

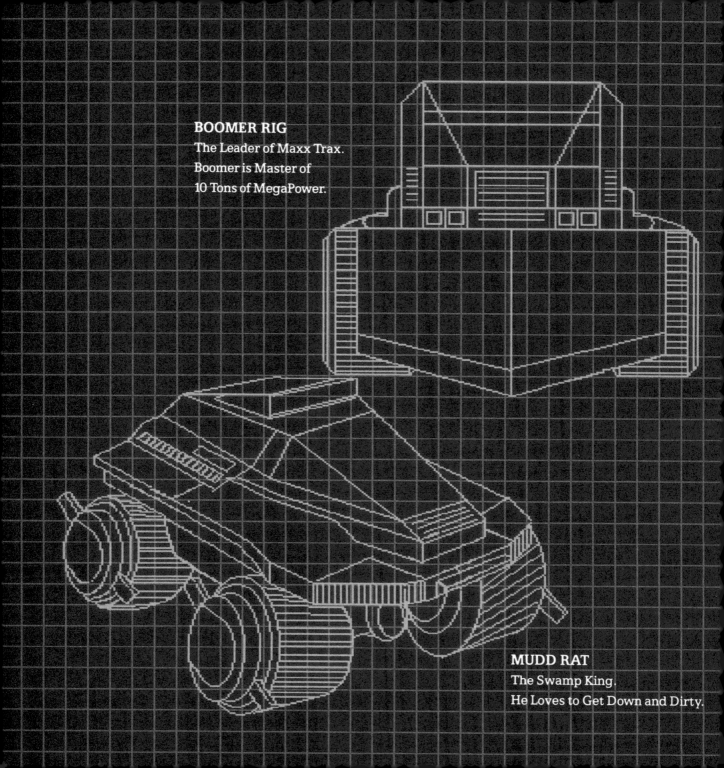

BOOMER RIG
The Leader of Maxx Trax.
Boomer is Master of
10 Tons of MegaPower.

MUDD RAT
The Swamp King.
He Loves to Get Down and Dirty.

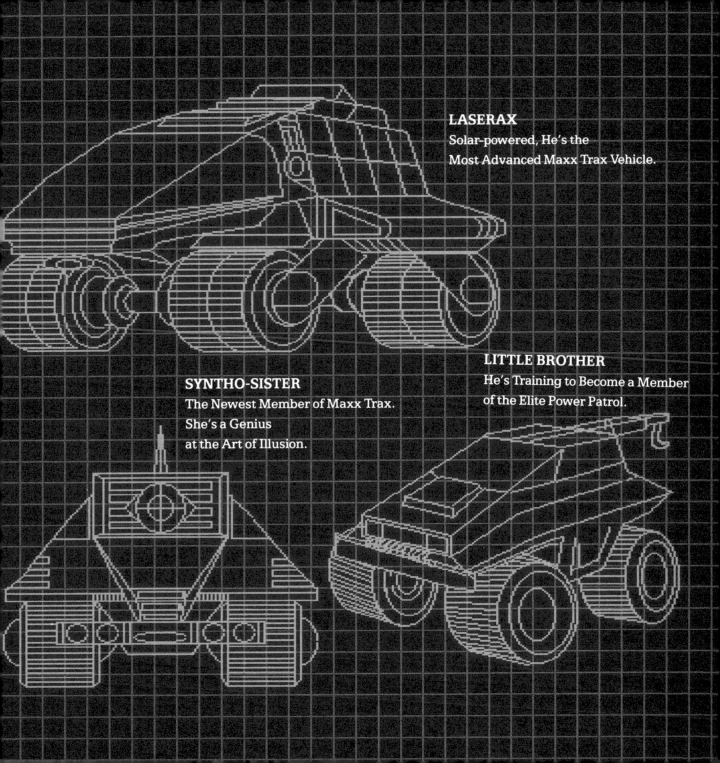

LASERAX
Solar-powered, He's the
Most Advanced Maxx Trax Vehicle.

SYNTHO-SISTER
The Newest Member of Maxx Trax.
She's a Genius
at the Art of Illusion.

LITTLE BROTHER
He's Training to Become a Member
of the Elite Power Patrol.

Boomer Rig, Mudd Rat, and Laserax raced over the mountains toward the Valley of Limestone. They were on their way to check on an important water project. Their friends, the gigantic Metalla-saurs, were building a reservoir that would serve all Maxx Trax facilities.

"Power Patrol, shift into All-Terrain gear!" Boomer ordered.

Mudd Rat's retractable steel wheel claws chewed up rocks and dirt as he roared up the mountain. Laserax blazed a trail with his multiple spray lasers. And Boomer, with his Earth-Mover Blades, plowed through everything in his way.

Back at Command Center, Little Brother and Syntho-Sister were monitoring the Patrol's activities.

Syntho-Sister, the newest Maxx Trax vehicle, equipped with the latest in video technology, was practicing her three-dimensional hologram projections.

"Watch, Little Brother," she said, as she projected Boomer Rig's image against a wall. It looked just like Boomer…but it was only a hologram image of him!

"Big deal," said Little Brother, who was a little jealous. "You can't tow like I can. Besides, we've got work to do."

But unknown danger lurked nearby. Evil Draxial and his dim-witted pal, Retread, were meeting in their secret cave.

"Uh...what are you thinking about, Duh—Duh—Draxial?" Retread asked.

"Oh, nothing, my little heap of spare parts," Draxial said. "Merely a brilliant plan to overthrow Boomer Rig and his so-called Power Patrol."

"But how can we defeat P—P—Power Patrol?" Retread asked.

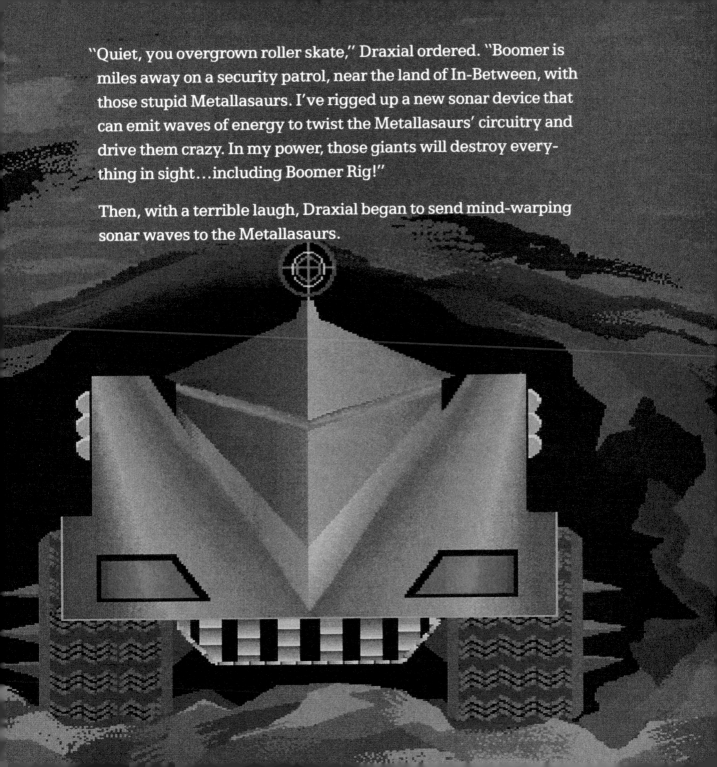

"Quiet, you overgrown roller skate," Draxial ordered. "Boomer is miles away on a security patrol, near the land of In-Between, with those stupid Metallasaurs. I've rigged up a new sonar device that can emit waves of energy to twist the Metallasaurs' circuitry and drive them crazy. In my power, those giants will destroy everything in sight...including Boomer Rig!"

Then, with a terrible laugh, Draxial began to send mind-warping sonar waves to the Metallasaurs.

The Metallasaurs were peacefully completing their work on the reservoir. These strange metallic creatures were the last lumbering giants in the land—bizarre mutants of another time and place. They hurt no one, and no one hurt them…until Draxial sent his sonar waves across the sky to the land of In-Between.

Suddenly, the Metallasaurs became crazed monsters. They ripped trees from the ground, blasted mountains, and began destroying the reservoir itself.

Back at Command Center, Little Brother and Syntho-Sister were monitoring the destruction on video screens. They radioed a warning to Boomer.

"We've got some big problems," Boomer said. "Move out, Power Patrol!"

Boomer, Mudd Rat, and Laserax met the crazed Metallasaurs by the edge of the reservoir, in the Valley of Limestone. "What's the matter with them?" asked Mudd Rat.

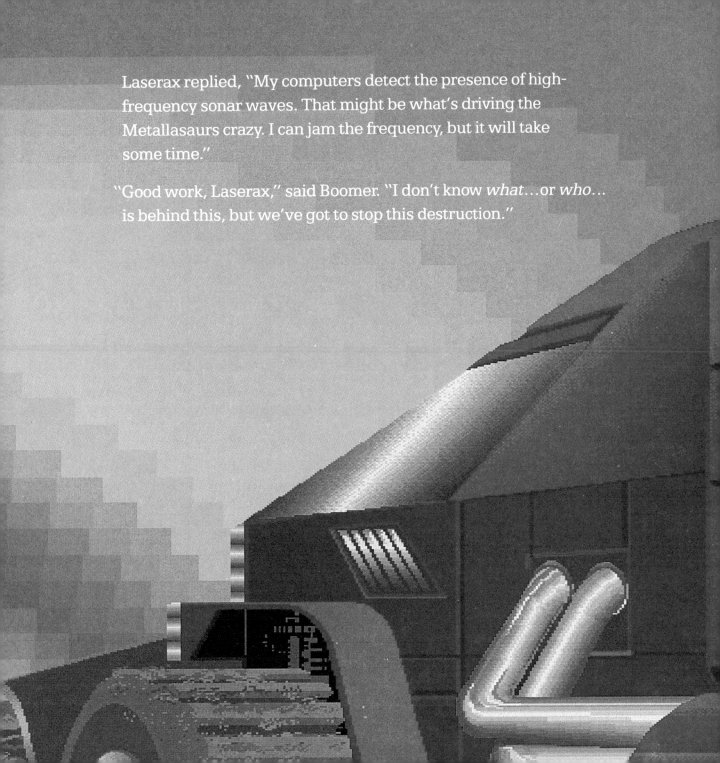

Laserax replied, "My computers detect the presence of high-frequency sonar waves. That might be what's driving the Metallasaurs crazy. I can jam the frequency, but it will take some time."

"Good work, Laserax," said Boomer. "I don't know *what*…or *who*… is behind this, but we've got to stop this destruction."

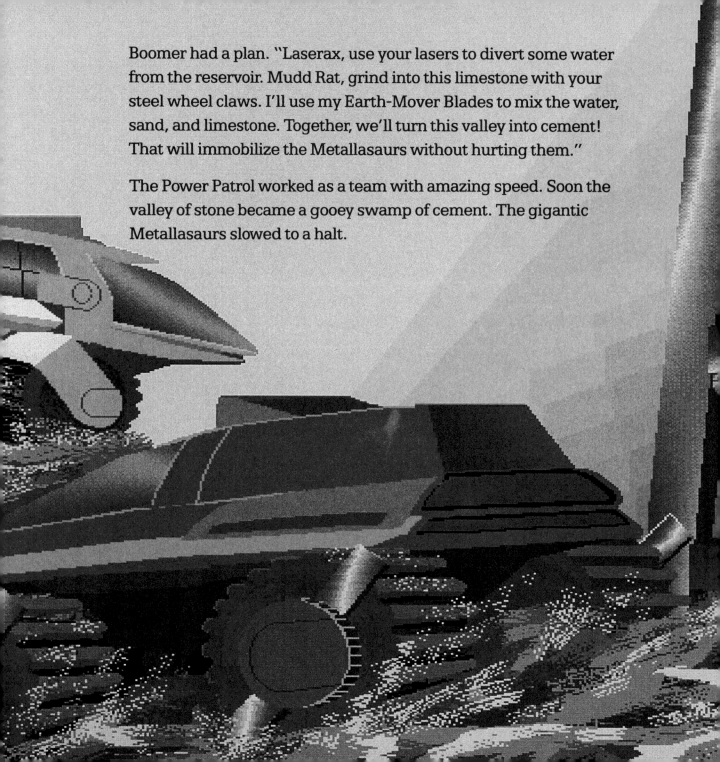

Boomer had a plan. "Laserax, use your lasers to divert some water from the reservoir. Mudd Rat, grind into this limestone with your steel wheel claws. I'll use my Earth-Mover Blades to mix the water, sand, and limestone. Together, we'll turn this valley into cement! That will immobilize the Metallasaurs without hurting them."

The Power Patrol worked as a team with amazing speed. Soon the valley of stone became a gooey swamp of cement. The gigantic Metallasaurs slowed to a halt.

Meanwhile, Little Brother and Syntho-Sister were having problems of their own. They had been captured by Draxial and chained to huge steel support columns in a Command Center storage facility.

"Now I am in Command!" Draxial shouted. "Even if Boomer Rig escapes the Metallasaurs, it will be impossible for you to warn him!"

"What are we gonna do now, Duh—Duh—Draxial?" Retread asked.

"Quiet, you metallic skateboard!" Draxial screamed. " I am in charge here. I have finally beaten the mighty Boomer Rig!"

Little Brother felt terrible. Boomer had left *him* in charge of Command Center. He thought everything was all his fault. "I've just got to warn Boomer," he said. Little Brother pulled at the chain with all his might. But it was no use. And even if he *could* escape, Draxial would still be in control of the Message Center. There would be no way to warn Boomer.

Then Little Brother had an idea. "Syntho-Sister," he called, "can you send a hologram message to Boomer?"

"Maybe," she answered, "but I have to be outdoors to do it. It might be possible to project a warning against a cloud in the sky. At least I can try!"

Little Brother knew that if he could just hook his towing winch to Syntho-Sister, they would have a fighting chance.

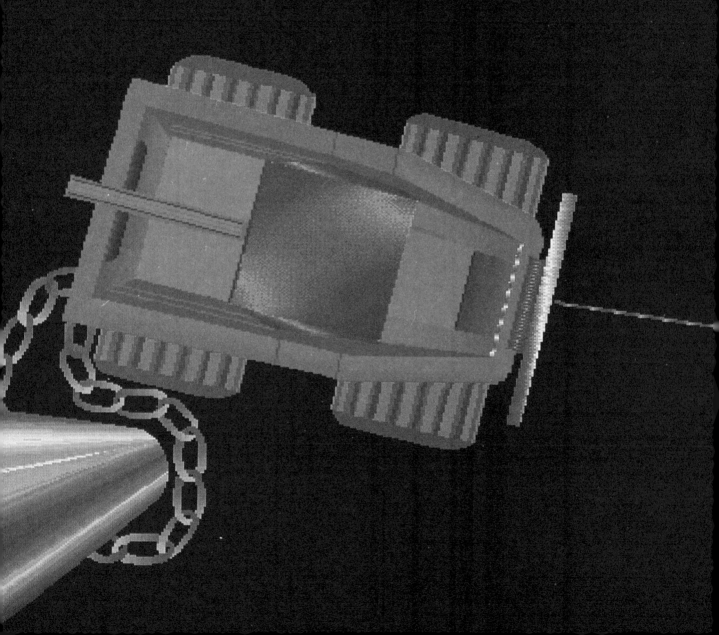

"There!" he cried as he hurled his towing winch cord and hooked it to Syntho-Sister. "Now, let's both pull, and pull hard. If we work together, maybe we can break your chain."

The two vehicles pulled as hard as they could. Slowly, the chain weakened. Finally…SNAP! Syntho-Sister was free!

"Quick," Little Brother told her. "Go out the back way and warn Boomer. You don't have much time, so step on it!"

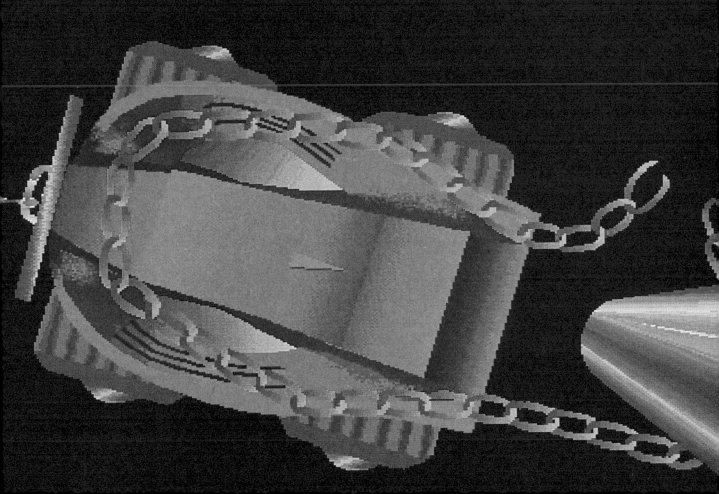

Boomer was checking the damage to the reservoir. Laserax had successfully jammed the sonar frequency. Once again, the Metallasaurs were functioning normally.

But as Power Patrol pulled the last Metallasaur out of the cement swamp, Boomer saw Syntho-Sister's warning in the sky. It was a 3-D hologram of Draxial—Boomer's arch enemy!

Boomer understood it instantly. "Power Patrol, Code Red!" he ordered. "We've got to get back to Command Center—PRONTO!"

Draxial was never so happy in all his rotten life. "All power is mine!" he roared. "Retread, bring Little Brother and Syntho-Sister to me. They will become my slaves."

"Not so fast, Draxial," a familiar voice called out. It was Boomer... and he had brought the Metallasaurs with him! They had a score to settle with evil Draxial.

"Yipes! M—M—Metallasaurs!" stammered Draxial and Retread.
They turned and tried to escape.

The mighty Metallasaurs reached down and grabbed the two villains. The giants lifted them up in their huge mouths and carried them away.

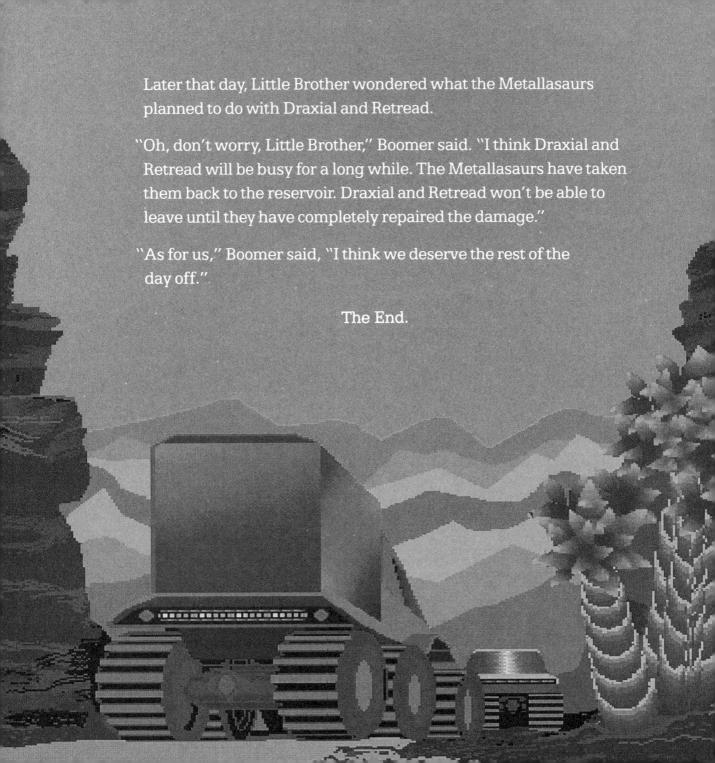

Later that day, Little Brother wondered what the Metallasaurs planned to do with Draxial and Retread.

"Oh, don't worry, Little Brother," Boomer said. "I think Draxial and Retread will be busy for a long while. The Metallasaurs have taken them back to the reservoir. Draxial and Retread won't be able to leave until they have completely repaired the damage."

"As for us," Boomer said, "I think we deserve the rest of the day off."

The End.